MAIL HARRY TO THE MOON!

Written by
Robie H. Harris

Pictures by
Michael Emberley

LITTLE, BROWN AND COMPANY
Books for Young Readers
New York   Boston

For my BIG brother, Peter!
Thanks for flying to the moon!
xx's, Your baby sister, Robie

For Becca, who,
as far as I remember,
never tried to mail me anywhere...

—M. E.

Little, Brown and Company

Hachette Book Group USA
237 Park Avenue, New York, NY 10017
Visit our Web site at www.lb-kids.com

First Edition: June 2008

ISBN-10: 0-316-15376-1
ISBN-13: 978-0-316-15376-8

10 9 8 7 6 5 4 3 2

TWP

Printed in Singapore

Book design by Maria Mercado

Before Harry was born,
there was **ME**!

ME

HARRY

ME

HARRY

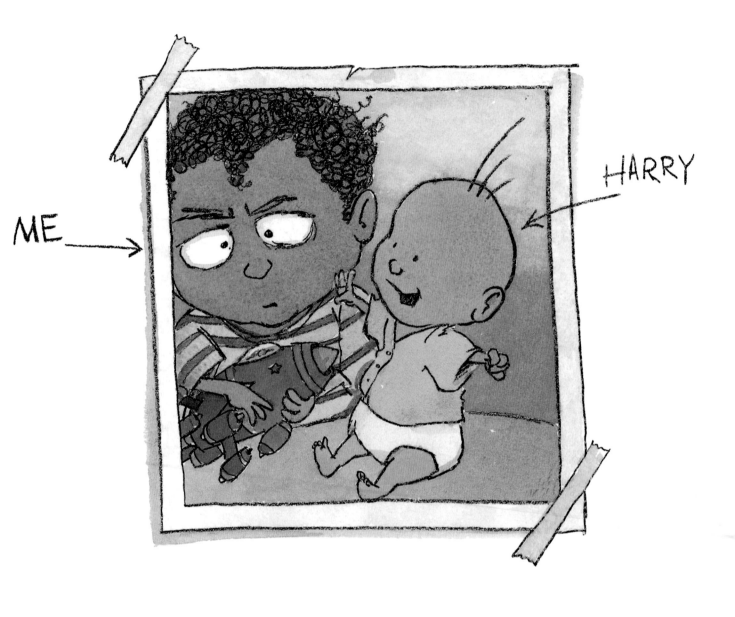

Now there's me.
And **Harry**.

Before Harry,
nobody took a bite of my banana.

Yesterday, Harry did.
So I said,

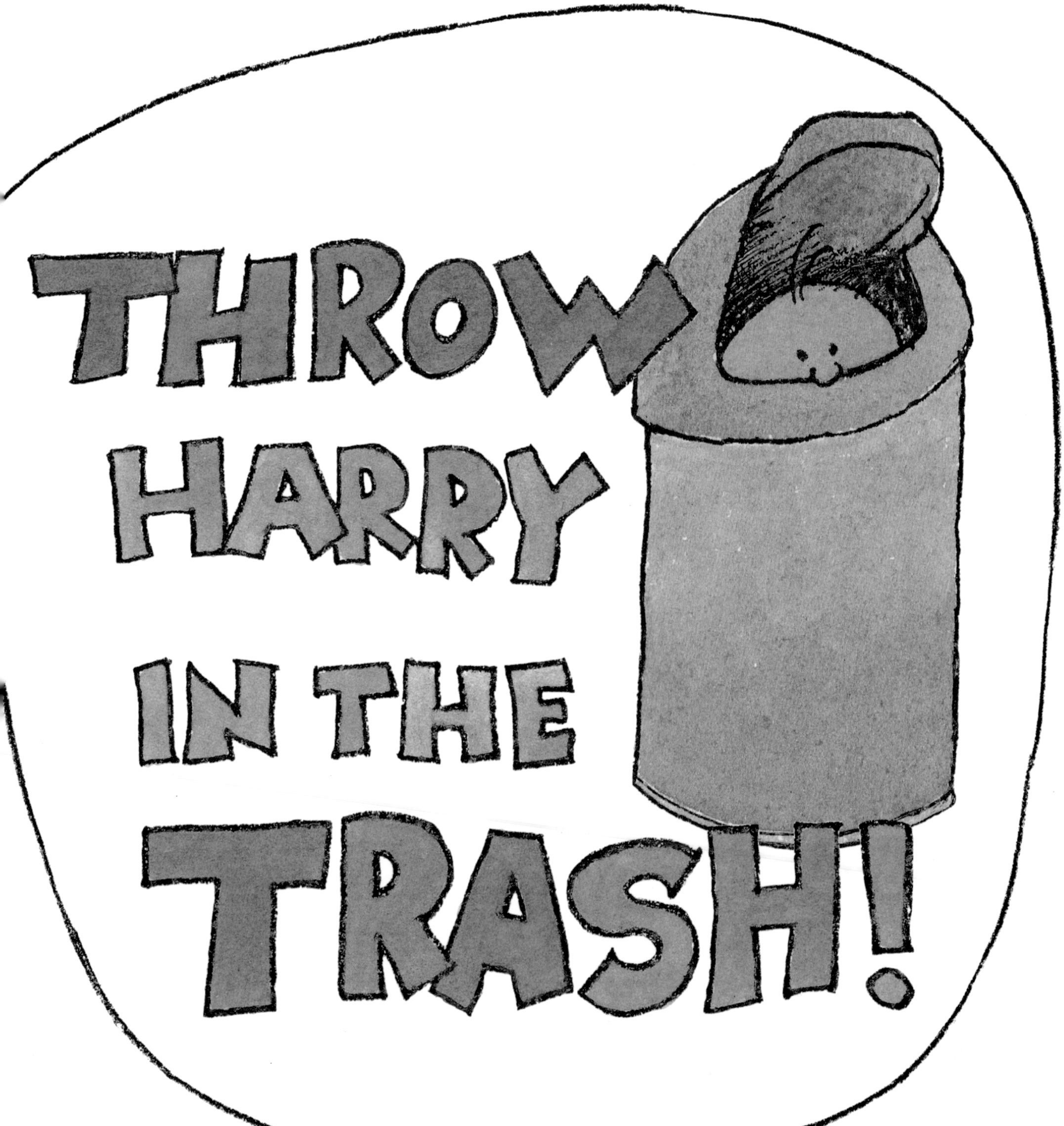
THROW
HARRY
IN THE
TRASH!

Before Harry,
nobody in my family spit up
smelly, yucky, cheesy stuff.

Yesterday, Harry did.

So I said,

FLUSH HARRY DOWN THE TOILET!

Before Harry,
nobody grabbed my gorilla
and chewed on its nose.

Yesterday, Harry did.

So I said,

Before Harry,
nobody but ME sat on Grandma's lap.

Yesterday, Harry did.
So I said,

Before Harry,
there was NO screaming baby
in our house.

Last night,
there WAS a screaming baby
in our house.

So I screamed right back,

MAIL H
TO THE
MO

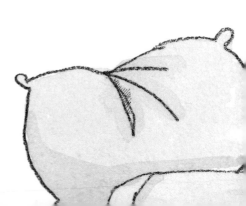

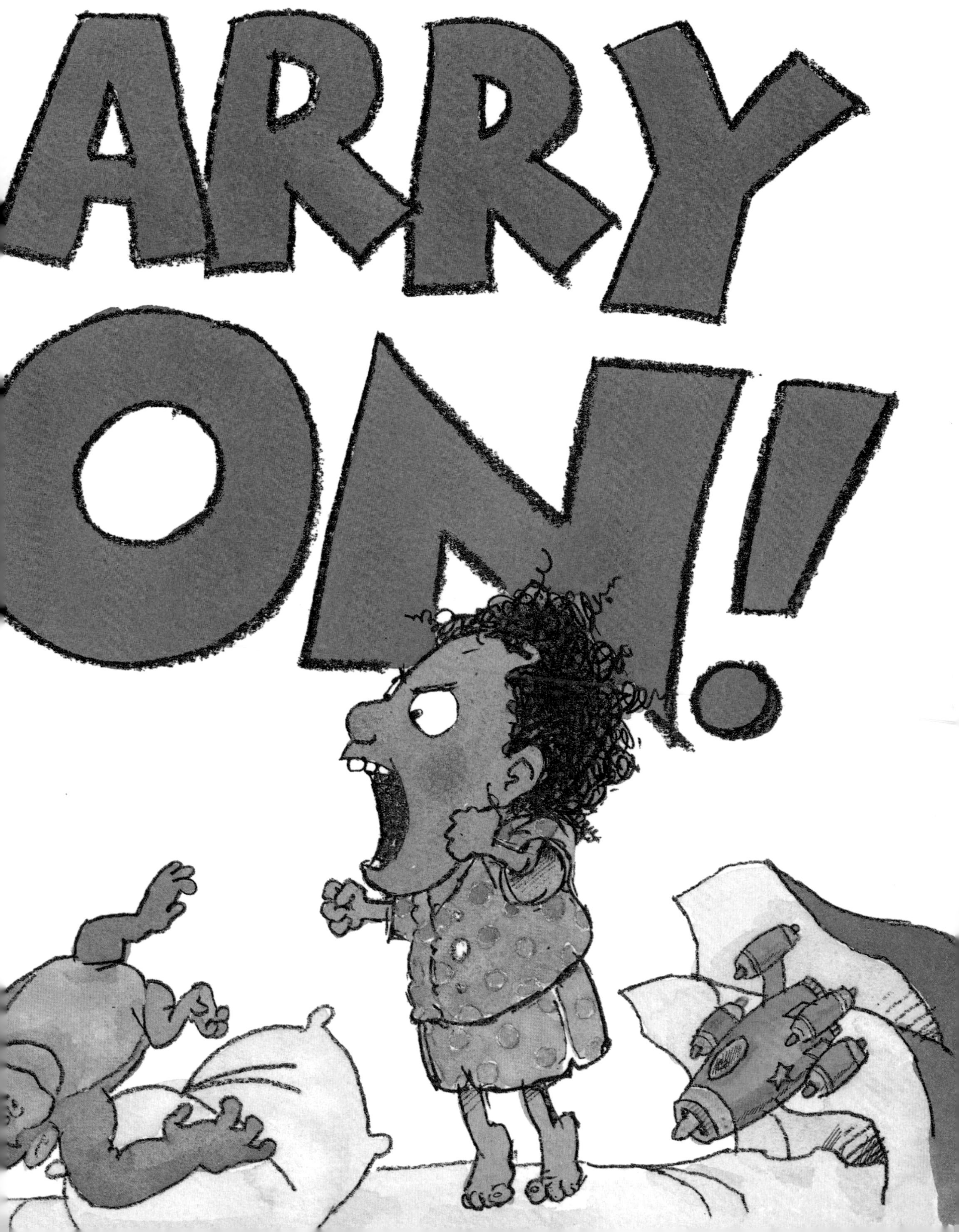
ARRY
ON!

This morning when I woke up,
there was no Harry screaming.

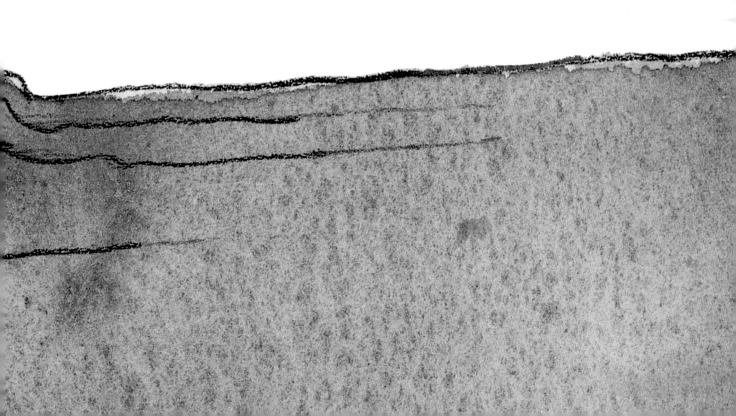

No Harry babbling.

No Harry burping.

There was no
Harry noise at all.

Hey Harry!
Are you in the trash?

Or in the toilet?

Inside Mommy?

In the zoo?

Harry?
Are you . . .

But Harry's too little to be
on the moon all by himself!
I had to go to the moon right away.

Soon I was on the moon!
And Harry was there.
He was so excited to see me,
he burped!

On the way home,
I let Harry sit on my lap and pat my gorilla.
Wasn't that nice of me?

We flew right through the clouds . . .

and straight through the front door . . .

. . . just in time for an afternoon snooze.

Before Harry was born—
there was **ME**.

Now there's ME **AND** HARRY!